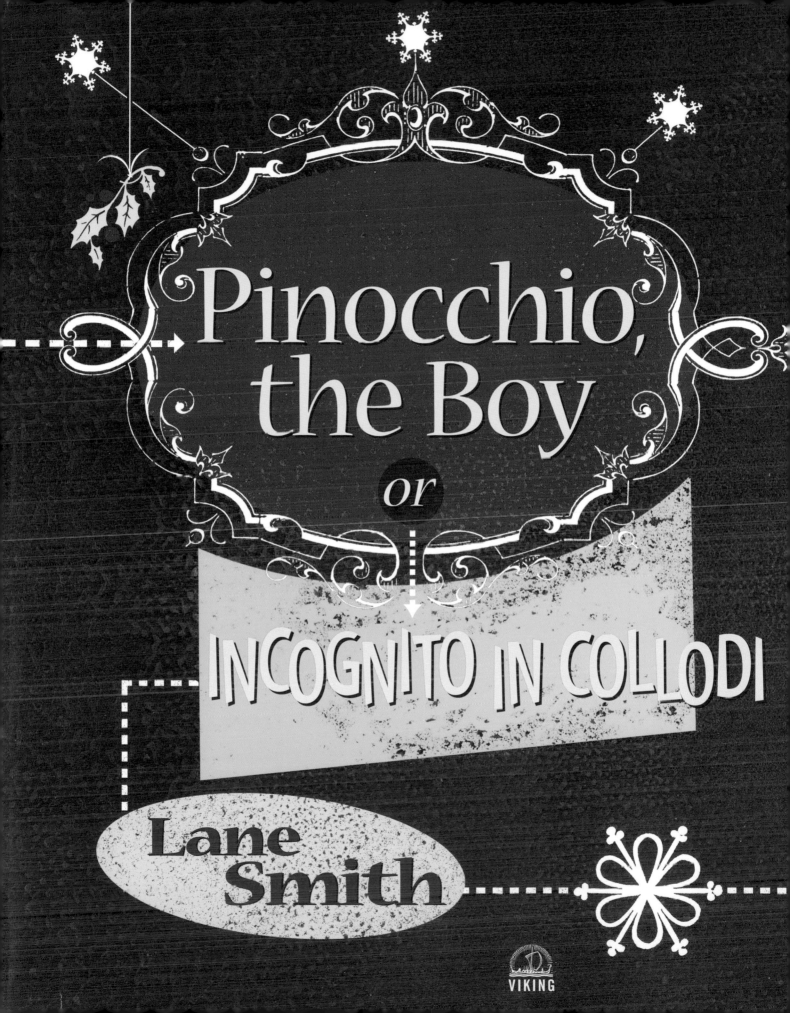

Pinocchio, the Boy

or

INCOGNITO IN COLLODI

Lane Smith

VIKING

To my mother,
who loves the snow.

VIKING
Published by the Penguin Group
Penguin Putnam Books for Young Readers, 345 Hudson Street, New York, New York 10014, U.S.A.
Penguin Books Ltd, Registered Offices: Harmondsworth, Middlesex, England

First published in 2002 by Viking, a division of Penguin Putnam Books for Young Readers.

10 9 8 7 6 5 4 3 2 1

LIBRARY OF CONGRESS CATALOGING-IN-PUBLICATION DATA
Smith, Lane
Pinocchio, the boy : incognito in Collodi / by Lane Smith
Summary: Pinocchio has been turned into a boy but no one, not even he, realizes
it as he walks through Collodi-town trying to get some hot chicken soup for Geppetto.
ISBN: 0-670-03585-8 (hardcover)
[1. Identity—Fiction. 2. Humorous stories.] I. Title.
PZ7.S65385 Pi 2002   [Fic] —dc21   2002001020

Printed In Mexico

Design by Molly Leach

LAST WEEK, in a nutshell...

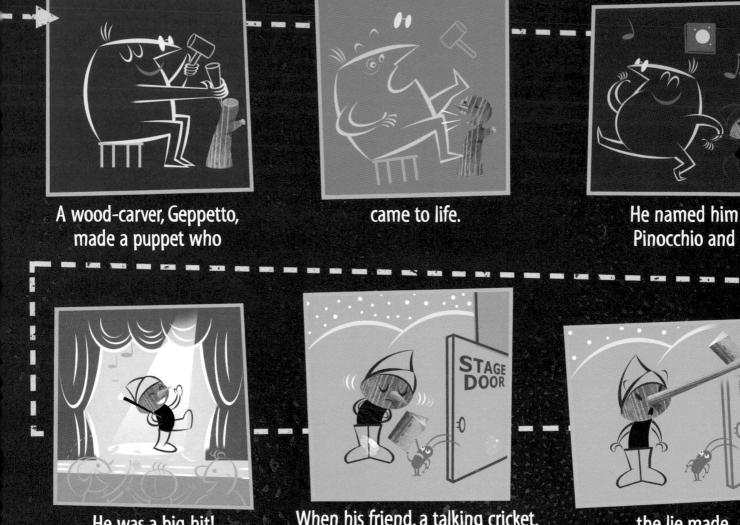

A wood-carver, Geppetto, made a puppet who

came to life.

He named him Pinocchio and

He was a big hit!

When his friend, a talking cricket, scolded him, Pinocchio lied and

the lie made his nose grow.

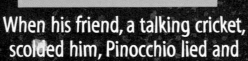

But Geppetto ended up in a Big Fish.

Pinocchio risked life and wooden limb to

save him and

sent him to school.

But Pinocchio went to

a puppet theater instead.

Ashamed, he
ran far away.

Geppetto searched
for him high and

low.

his good deed was
rewarded with a
visit from the Blue
Fairy, who came to
grant his one and
only wish.

And so, with a wave of her wand, the Blue Fairy granted this wish and turned the wooden puppet Pinocchio into . . .

. . . a real boy.

But he had no idea! That nutty fairy had changed him while he was asleep.

Here he is waking up. Next to him is Geppetto, still sleeping.
Geppetto is sick and wet from that fish's belly.

Pinocchio checked his father's temperature. 104°!
Maybe some chicken soup would help.

In the cupboard, he didn't see any soup.

And in the mirror,
he didn't see that he was now a boy.

So off to Collodi City for hot chicken soup to—

"Nuts. No money."

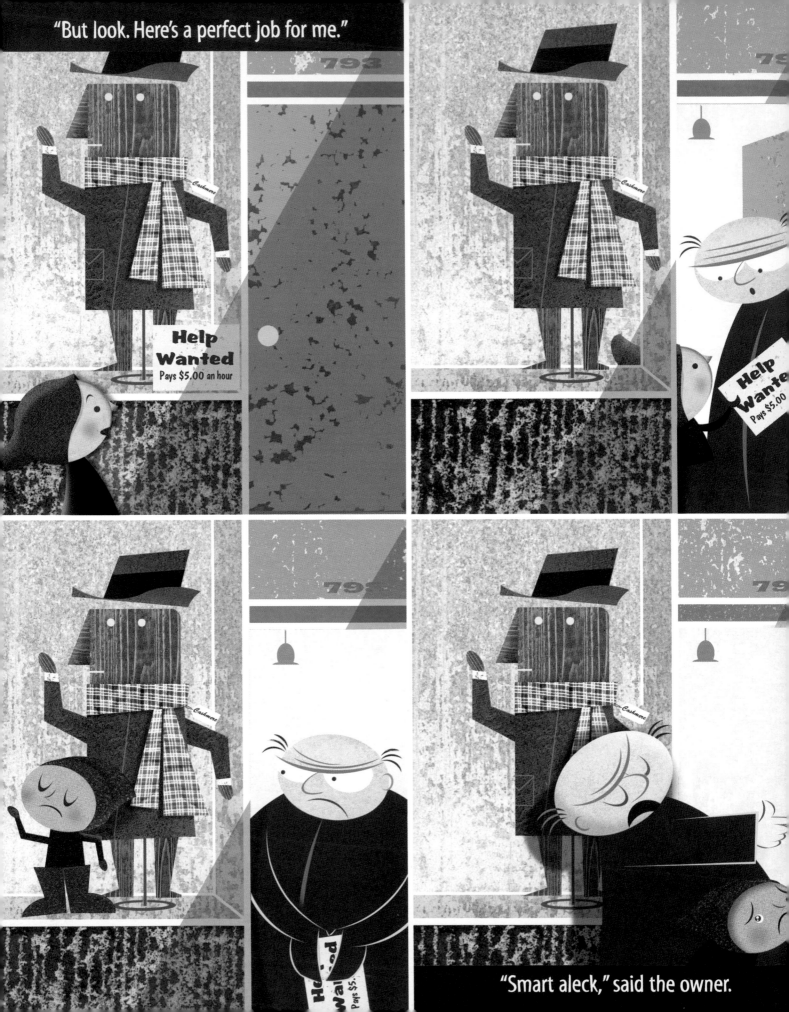

"He probably doesn't see too many wooden boys," thought Pinocchio.
"If only Cricket were here. He'd know what to—

Cricket always helped Pinocchio when he was confused. But Cricket knew only a
puppet of knotty pine. Not a flesh-and-blood boy. So when Pinocchio asked for his help

. . . Cricket just said *crick, crick, crick* as he crawled away.

The girl followed Pinocchio. She wanted to see what this funny bo

...vould do next.

"Will you give me five dollars for my special hankie?" he asked.

"Let's see this 'special hankie,'" said the shopkeeper.

The girl caught up with Pinocchio. "Talking bugs? A long nose?" she said.
"What will you think of next?"

"I just thought of it," he said.

Pinocchio went to the puppet theater where just last week he was a Big Sensation.

He hopped on the stage and did "The March of the Wooden Soldier" and "The Dance of the Marionette." And the audience . . .

...flat on his back.

"Strike three," said the girl.

"What's happening? My cricket doesn't talk to me, I can't get a job, and my dad's sick at home from spending the night in a fish."

"At least your dad *is* home," said the girl. "My mom is so busy I hardly ever see her."

Pinocchio felt he had let his father down. After a whole day he had no soup and no new ideas.

He wished he could talk to his dad—but wait! Was that Geppetto talking to *him*?
He looked up and there, on a big TV screen, was ...

Geppetto, what else
can you tell us
about your son?

Well, he's about so high . . .
red cap . . . red boots . . .

4:05
26°
LIVE 3

Pinocchio, where are
you? Please come home!

4:05
26°
LIVE 3

I'm feeling much better
since this nice lad

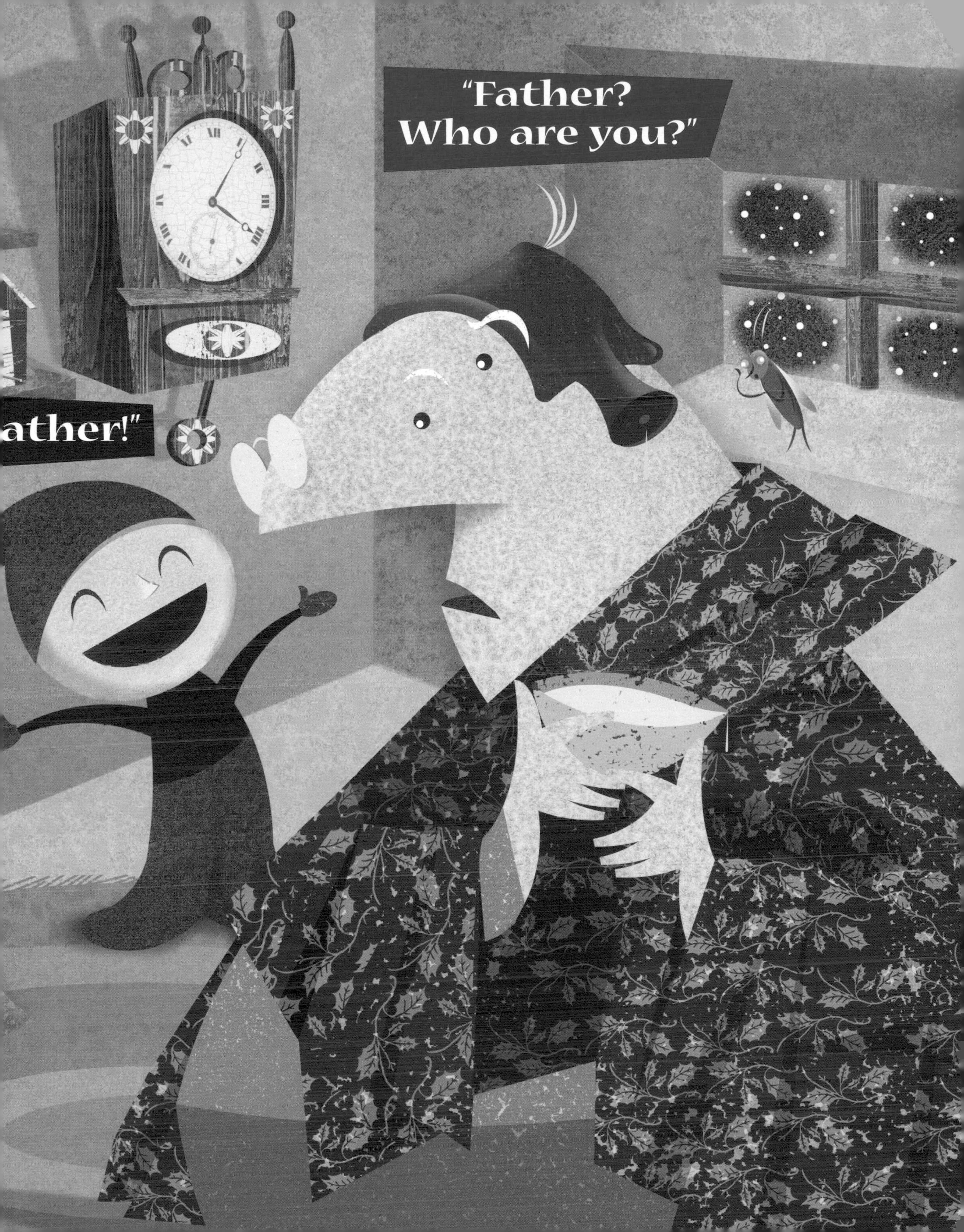
"Father?
Who are you?"
ather!"

. . . RIGHT HERE.

That's when the Blue Fairy jumped in. "I guess this is all my fault," she said.
"Last night, while you were sleeping, I waved my little wand and, silly me, turned you into a real . . .

"Boy!"
shouted
Pinocchio.

Then, to make up for her little slip, the Blue Fair

treated everyone to an evening at Collodi Rink.

Later, the girl and her mother headed home. "You never told me you were a *fairy*," said the girl. "No wonder you're so busy." The Blue Fairy just smiled at her daughter, Hershabel.

"But mom," continued Hershabel, "next time you change a puppet into a kid, you might want to wake him first."